WOODLAN: TALES

By Rene Cloke

AWARD PUBLICATIONS LIMITED

ISBN 0-86163-534-5

Copyright © 1991 Award Publications Limited

First published 1991
Reprinted 1993

Published by Award Publications Limited,
1st Floor, Goodyear House,
52-56 Osnaburgh street,
London NW1 3NS

Printed in Belgium.

CONTENTS

Mandy's Umbrella

Mandy, the woodmouse, picked up the letter
that had just arrived in the mail.

It was big and white and looked
very exciting.

"I will get my breakfast ready first,"
she decided and propped the letter
against the butter dish.

Then she sat down
at the breakfast table
and opened the envelope.

"Dear Mandy," she read,
"A few friends are coming
to lunch with me on Friday;
I shall be so pleased if
you are able to join us.

With love, Meg."

Mandy was delighted.
"I will wear my new dress and hat; I do hope it will be a sunny day."

But Friday was not a bright day.

It was raining and the wind was blowing
through the trees.

Mandy put on her new dress and her new hat;
she looked very pretty as she started off
through the woods with her big umbrella.

The wind was blowing so hard that Mandy could hardly keep her umbrella over her head.

"Oh dear! This is terrible!" she squeaked, and then a great gust of wind pulled the umbrella out of her paw and carried it off over the trees.

"How shall I keep dry?" moaned poor Mandy. "My pretty new hat will be ruined."

And then she saw a large mushroom. "That will do beautifully!" she cried picking up the mushroom and, holding it over her head, she hurried along.

Mandy stopped at the little woodland shop
and looked in the window.
"I will buy some sweets for Meg,"
she decided and, leaving
her mushroom umbrella on the porch,
she went into the shop.

As usual the shop was full of customers.
Belinda Bunny sold everything that anyone could want and she was very busy behind the counter.
Mr. Spindle was buying a bucket and duster and Mrs. Moley wanted some apples.
The young squirrels were choosing bars of chocolate and packets of biscuits and Mrs. Dora Quack-duck was asking for a loaf of bread and some butter.

It was quite a long time before Mandy could get served. She chose a box of mixed toffees for her friend and Belinda wrapped it in pretty paper.

When Mandy walked out of the shop with her package she looked around for her mushroom umbrella – it had disappeared!

Perhaps it had blown away
like her real umbrella.
    "Oh well," she said,
"it has stopped raining,
so I will hurry along
as quickly as I can.
Meg's house isn't too far."

15

When she arrived at the little house in the
hollow tree she was greeted by all her friends,
Flippy Frog, Filbert and Sally Squirrel,
Woody Vole and Noddy Dormouse.

"Come in!" cried Meg. "I am just going to make omelettes for lunch."

Everyone sat down at the table and
Meg brought in a big dish of omelettes.
  "I was very lucky," she told them,
"as I passed the shop this morning,
I saw a big mushroom outside,
so I cut it up and put it
in the omelettes."

"Why, that was my umbrella,"
cried Mandy, "and
we are eating it!"

Everyone laughed and
Mandy told them about
her real umbrella
blowing away.

"I know where it is,"
said Flippy, "it flew
past me this morning
and was caught in a tree
near my house."

So, after lunch,
all the animals went to look
for the lost umbrella.

There it was,
high in the branches
of a tree.
   "It's a long way up,"
said Mandy, "I wonder
if I can climb
up there."

"I'll get it for you,"
said Filbert and he
scurried up the tree.
  Since he was a very good
climber, he was soon able
to rescue the umbrella
and give it back
to Mandy.

The animals waved goodbye to Mandy
as she hurried home.

"A good end to your adventures," they cried,
"don't lose your umbrella again
and don't let anyone eat it!"

But Mandy's adventures were not over.

When she reached her house, she found that the rain had left a deep pool all around the tree, right up to the doorstep.

It looked deep
and very cold.

"I don't want to get wet swimming across that,"
she said anxiously. "Now what shall I do?
I wish I had a little boat and then I could row
across to my house."
Then she had a bright idea.

She opened her umbrella and
rested it on the water.
Then she stepped gently inside and,
taking a little stick,
she pushed off
from the bank.
The umbrella was like
a real little boat.

It was a rocky ride and once the umbrella
was caught in a tuft of grass.

At last, she made her way across the pond
and reached her house.

There was some water in her umbrella but Mandy
tipped it back into the pond before she
opened the door.

"There," she said as she crept up the step
and through the door, "safely home again
and my umbrella has been very useful after all."
    She hung it up on a peg and took off her
hat and coat.
    "Oh, dear! I am quite tired."

She made herself a cup of tea,
put some little cakes on a tray and
went up to bed.

Very soon she was fast asleep and dreaming about
sailing across a huge pond in a little boat
that kept changing into an umbrella
and then into a big mushroom.

Mandy was quite glad to wake up and find her umbrella still hanging on the peg.

"Next time it rains," she said, "I will tie it to my paw."

Spindle's Picnic

Spindle Hedgehog lived in a
cosy little house in the root of
a tree on the edge of Oaktree Wood.
"It's a fine sunny day," he said, looking out of
the door one morning, "I'll take a picnic
down to the river."

He cut some sandwiches,
packed some cheese and biscuits
and an orange.

"I think that will be enough,"
he decided.

Spindle put the packet into the carrier
of his bicycle, put on his jacket and scarf
and rode off through the woods
towards the river.

"A lovely day for a ride." called Mandy Mouse as he rode past her house, "Have a good time."

Then he met Filbert and Sally Squirrel
who were looking very worried.
"We've lost little Frisky," they told him, "he didn't
come home yesterday evening and he has been
out all night."
"I hope he hasn't fallen into the river," said Sally,
"he hasn't yet learnt how to swim."

34

"I'm going down to the river,"
Spindle told them, "I'll keep
a sharp look-out for him.
I expect he has lost his way
in the woods."

When Spindle reached the river, he propped his bicycle against a tree and went down to the water's edge.

"How cool and fresh the water looks," he said, "I think I'll have a paddle before I eat my lunch."

He wandered up the river and on his way back
saw Winnie Water-vole carrying a heavy basket
on her way home from the woodland shop.

"Oh, dear! How tired I am!" she sighed.

"Would you like to borrow my bicycle?"
suggested Spindle. "You could hang your basket
on the handlebar. I don't mind walking home."

Winnie was very grateful
and rode off on Spindle's bicycle
with her shopping.
The hedgehog sat in the sun
to dry his feet and then he thought
about his lunch.

"Oh, how stupid I am!" he cried. "I've left my picnic lunch in the carrier of my bicycle."

Then he thought hard.

"I'd better walk along through the woods to the shop and see what I can buy; I'm afraid I haven't much money in my pocket."

Spindle put on his jacket and his shoes and socks and walked off through the trees to the little shop kept by Belinda Bunny.

He felt very hungry and bought a pie and an apple.

There were a great many people in the shop
and Spindle asked if any of them had seen
little Frisky Squirrel.

Everyone said "No," but promised to look out for him.

As Spindle walked back
to the river he heard
a little squeak and there,
in the rushes, with his foot caught
between two rocks, was little Frisky
looking very wet and uncomfortable.

"Help! help!" he cried.
"I can't get my foot free!
I crawled along that branch
to pick some nuts
and I fell off into the river
and got caught in the
rocks."

Spindle put down his bag of shopping, took off
his jacket and his shoes and socks and waded
into the river.

"I'm coming," he called out to Frisky.

He soon reached the little squirrel
and managed to move the big stone
and get the foot free.

Together they waded back to the shore
and sat down on the grass to dry their
wet feet and legs.

44

"I'm so hungry," whimpered the little squirrel, "I lost my way in the woods when it got dark and I didn't have any supper last night or any breakfast this morning. I don't know what time it is but I don't think I'll have any lunch today."

Spindle looked at his pie and his apple.

He was hungry, too, but he was a kind
little hedgehog and gave the pie to Frisky
and took just one bite from the apple.
Charlie Chaffinch hoped that
there might be something for him.

"Now we must hurry home," said Spindle, when Frisky had eaten every crumb, "it is getting dark and everyone is very worried about you."

Frisky was so tired that Spindle offered to carry him on his back, but the hedgehog was so covered with spines that Frisky found it wasn't very comfortable.

Filbert and Sally
were delighted to
see them and young Frisky
had a long story
to tell about his
adventures.

"But first of all,"
declared Sally, "you must
both come in and have
a good meal.
Tea is ready!"

Oh, it was a lovely tea!
There was a big dish of eggs and mushrooms,
plenty of cakes, bread and butter and a
lovely apple pie with cream.

All the squirrel family gathered round
the table and Spindle and Frisky were given
big helpings of everything until they
simply couldn't eat any more!

Then they sat around the fire and Frisky
told them all about his wanderings in the
dark woods last night and about the way Spindle
had rescued him from the river and
given him his pie and his apple.

At last, Spindle said "Goodnight," waved goodbye to the squirrels and hurried home.

"Well," he murmured as he crept into bed, "I didn't have my picnic sandwiches and I didn't have my pie but that lovely tea made up for missing them!" and he fell asleep dreaming about rescuing little squirrels and apples and oranges from the river.

Next day there was a surprise present for him on the doorstep.

A big basket of fruit from Filbert and Sally with a little note to thank him for his kindness to young Frisky.

Vicky's New Hat

Vicky, the fox cub, was very excited.

"I have been asked to look after the flower stall at the bazaar tomorrow," she told her friends in Oaktree Wood.

"Money is being collected for the baby animals' holiday-treat."

"What fun!" cried Rusty Rabbit,
"We'll all go to the bazaar."
"We will collect some flowers
for you," said Filbert and
Sally Squirrel.
"Thank you," said Vicky,
"my new hat will be
just right for a flower stall;
I will put it on
and you shall all see it."

Vicky fetched her new hat.
All the animals thought
it was beautiful – but,

– a sharp wind blew it from
Vicky's head and it
floated off over the grass.

"Oh, catch it, catch it!" cried Vicky.
They all chased it but they were
not quick enough; the beautiful hat
blew into the river.

The ducks dragged it out
of the river. The wonderful
hat was ruined.
Vicky was very sad.

"I shall have to wear my
old hat," she said,
"this one is soaked," and she
walked off with it dangling
from her paw.

"Let's try to make a
fine new hat for Vicky,"
suggested Rusty,
"I'll collect some
rushes to plait
together."

"I'll find some flowers to decorate it," said Filbert.

"And here are some pretty feathers," said
Penny Pigeon.

Flippy Frog helped Rusty to gather some rushes and,
together, they wove them into a bright little
green hat.

The squirrels and Mandy Mouse made a daisy-chain and picked a bunch of forget-me-nots and buttercups to trim the hat. Then they fastened the little feathers at the side.

"I hope it's the right size," said Filbert, "it looks very pretty."

It was and Vicky was delighted.

She started off for the bazaar with two huge baskets of flowers, one on each arm. The little hat was perched on her head and she wore a new blue dress.

"Goodbye!" she cried. "And thank you all very much."

The others waved goodbye as she walked through the trees.

"Sell all the flowers!" cried Mandy Mouse.

"And don't let your hat blow off again!" called Rusty.

The bazaar was held in a little glade in the middle of the woods.

Vicky arrived in good time to set up her stall.

She put bunches of flowers in bowls and vases and made buttonholes and garlands for people who wanted flowers to wear.

Then she decorated the stall with trails of ivy, creeper and pine-cones and set the pot plants on the ground.

Everyone said it looked beautiful and Vicky felt very pleased.

She had time to walk around and look at the other stalls.

There were stalls full of clothes, tea-cosies and egg-cosies and all kinds of pretty things.

Belinda and Billy Bunny had jars of sweets
and boxes of chocolates as well as toffee,
fruit and cakes on their stall.
Some of the toffee had not hardened very well,
so while Billy was wrapping it up in small
bargain packets; quite a lot of it stuck
to his paws!

At three o'clock,
the bazaar was opened by
the famous Miss Gwen Goose
who was well known for her
beautiful paintings of
farmyard scenes.

"I am sure everything will
be sold," she said, "and I would
like to thank you for the lovely
bouquet you have given me,"
and she waved the bunch of
flowers to show that everyone
could begin to sell and buy.

There was much clapping and cheering and Miss Goose bowed and curtsied.

The animals gathered round the stalls; some tried their luck in the bran-tub and some tried guessing the weight of an enormous cake that Billy Bunny pushed around in his wheelbarrow.

There was a tent where tea was served and a stall for ices and fruit drinks.
Then the sports began.

Rusty Rabbit was winning the egg and spoon race easily.
Suddenly he stepped on a piece of the sticky toffee and couldn't run any further but he slipped off his shoe, ran on, and came in first after all.

Some animals said that Flippy Frog shouldn't have been allowed in the sack race because he was too good at hopping. But, since he was the smallest in the race, he was allowed to take the prize.

The three-legged race was the most exciting.
No one seemed to be able to run straight and
just as Sally and Filbert Squirrel were passing
Vicky's stall they lost their balance –
Crash! Over went the stall!
Over went the vases and all the lovely flowers
were broken and scattered on the ground.

Everyone ran to help
the squirrels and the
flowers were trampled on.
"Oh, dear!" moaned Vicky.
"All my flowers will be
crushed and broken and I won't
have any money to give
to the bazaar."

She tried to pick them up and to collect the vases
that were not broken but the excited animals stepped
on her paws and at last she gave it up.
    She wandered off to a quiet corner and,
sitting down by a water-lily pond,
she sobbed and sobbed.

No one noticed her for a long time. Vicky was
quite startled when she heard a kind voice cackle -
"Why, what is the matter?
Have you hurt yourself?"

Vicky looked up
and there was the famous
Miss Gwen Goose bending over her,
holding, under one wing,
her bouquet of flowers.

She looked so kind that Vicky told her
all about the flower stall.

"Well, well!" said Miss Goose. "This is a
sad tale, but we'll soon fix everything!"

She held out a wing to Vicky and the
little cub clutched it eagerly.

"Come with me and I'll see what can be done."

They hurried off to the busy glade where
the stalls were set up.

73

The little rabbits and squirrels
helped to put up the stall again and
cleared away the crushed
flowers. Soon everything
was tidy.

"Now," said Miss Gwen Goose,
"we will arrange my lovely
bouquet into buttonholes and posies
and see if we can sell them all!"

74

Vicky thought this was
a splendid idea.
    They had so many customers
that in ten minutes
every flower was sold
and Vicky's money box
was so full that it
wouldn't even jingle!

And that was not the end of the excitement.
There was a grand parade of the stallholders
and a prize for the prettiest hat.
"The prize goes to Vicky the fox cub,"
called out the judge and he
presented Vicky with a
big box of chocolates.

"Plenty to share with all those who have helped me," said Vicky delightedly.

Barnaby's Cuckoo Clock

The tiny shop among the roots of the oak tree
in Hopping Wood belonged to Barnaby and
Bertha Bunny.

Barnaby picked up a letter from the mat one
morning and read it as he sat at breakfast
in the room behind the shop.

"Dear me!" he said. "Here is a letter from my
Aunt Brown-paws. She is coming to see us today
and will arrive on the bus at three o'clock."

"She will want to hear the cuckoo clock
she gave us for a wedding present six years ago,"
said Bertha, "and it hasn't 'cuckoo-ed' since
young Flip put the cuckoo in the bath."

"It wouldn't float at all," grumbled Flip.

"She will be very annoyed," said Barnaby. "I wonder if I can get it mended before she comes."

He took the clock from the wall and looked at it. It was a pretty clock, with acorns and flowers carved in wood around its painted blue face.

"I'll take it along to old Prickles and see if he can mend it," said Barnaby. The clock was heavy, so he put it in a wheelbarrow and trundled off to find Prickles.

Old Prickles, the hedgehog, looked at the clock and rubbed his head because he was puzzled.

"The clock is working," he said, "but the little bird doesn't jump out."

"I can mend watches and clocks and also clean them. I can even make new springs, but making little birds pop out and say 'cuckoo!' is a thing I never learned to do. It doesn't seem natural to me."

Meanwhile Bertha Bunny was very busy.
She took some flour, currants, butter, sugar and
a large pot of raspberry jam from the shelf
in her shop.
    She also took a loaf of bread and a pot of paste
for sandwiches.

"Now, Flip and Flop," Bertha told her two young bunnies, "You must mind the shop while I make some cakes and jam tarts for Aunt Brown-paws' tea. Be polite to the customers and keep the shop tidy."

She got out her rolling pin and pastry board and set to work.

Flip and Flop thought it was
great fun serving the customers.
They popped extra sweets into
the bags for their friends, Dumpling,
the black piglet and Merry,
the kitten, from Hopping Wood
Farm.

"I want some very tall candles," said Flipperty Frog, "you know, the sort that will stand well out of the water in my dining room." Hazel and Tufty Squirrel had come to buy a checked tablecloth and Flop had to climb the stepladder to get one from the shelf.

The stepladder wobbled and down fell
poor Flop straight into a barrel full of apples.
"Help!" shouted the little rabbit as the
barrel tipped over and all the apples were
scattered about the floor.

Dumpling pulled Flop up to his feet.
Larry, the puppy, and Merry collected the apples.
Then, everyone had a glass of lemonade,
to help them to recover from the shock of it all.
Dumpling had a biscuit as well, because
he said the accident had made him feel quite weak.

Barnaby walked slowly home with the cuckoo clock that wouldn't 'cuckoo'.

"Aunt Brown-paws will think we have been very careless with her present," he kept muttering. Then, as he pushed the wheelbarrow along through the wood, a voice called out to him . . .

"Hello, Barnaby! Taking your clock for a ride?"

Down from the branches of a thorn tree
hopped Charley Cuckoo and his friend Willie Wren.
Barnaby told them about the clock.
"The works are all right," he explained,
"but the bird doesn't 'cuckoo' when it pops out."

Charley looked very wise.
"I have an idea," he said.
"I will crouch on top of the
clock and call 'cuckoo! at the
right time and Willie will pop out
in place of the little wooden bird.
I'm sure your Aunt Brown-paws
won't know the difference."

"Splendid!" cried Barnaby
and they all hurried along to tell
Bertha about the grand plan.

Bertha wasn't too sure about the grand plan.

"It might work," she told them, "but Aunt Brown-paws will be very cross if she finds out."

"If the bus arrives at three o'clock and she leaves by the last bus at a quarter past four, we shall have to do it only once," said Willie.

"If you can do it without being discovered, I will give you each a jam tart," said Bertha.

So, they all bustled about and tidied the
burrow which was their home.
  Flip and Flop laid the lace table cloth and
Bertha brought out her best tea set.
She put all the tarts and cakes she had made
upon the table.

Barnaby hung the clock high up on the wall
so that Charley couldn't be seen sitting on the top.
Willie crept inside the clock and closed the little door.
   "Now!" cried Flip, who wanted to practise.
"It's just on three o'clock."
   Out popped Willie.
   Charlie Cuckoo cried: "Cuckoo!
Cuckoo! Cuckoo!"
   Willie popped back inside the clock and closed the
little wooden door.
   "That was wonderful!"
exclaimed Barnaby, full of
admiration.

Aunt Brown-paws arrived a few minutes later.
She was a very stately old rabbit and
everyone felt a bit afraid of her grand manner.
"Well," she said as she looked at the
cuckoo clock on the wall, "I'm glad to see that the
wedding present I gave you is keeping such
good time. I shall look forward to
hearing it at four o'clock.

I must leave you at four
to catch the last bus,"
Aunt Brown-paws added.
Flop giggled and pushed Flip,
who tumbled over and nearly
tripped up Bertha as she carried in the teapot.

Barnaby pretended that the little bunnies
were trying to show Aunt Brown-paws some
tricks and so they both turned somersaults
and stood on their heads. Aunt Brown-paws
looked a bit surprised and said she thought
the burrow was too small for games like that.

Then, Aunt Brown-paws poked her whiskers into Bertha's shop and said that it wasn't kept very tidily. Of course, there had been no time to tidy up after Flop's adventure with the apples.

"Come and have tea," said Bertha before Aunt Brown-paws had time to find fault with anything else.

So, they all sat down.
Bertha worried whether she had
remembered to put sugar in the
cakes and whether there was
enough jam in the tarts.

But she need not have worried.
Aunt Brown-paws was enjoying
her tea.

She ate four pieces of bread and butter, three sandwiches, two slices of currant cake and a jam tart.

"Do have another jam tart," said Barnaby politely. Aunt Brown-paws looked at the two tarts that were left on the table.

"They do taste good!" she said.

"Perhaps I . . ." Aunt Brown-paws was
interrupted.

"Cuckoo! Cuckoo! Cuckoo! Cuckoo!"

They all jumped and looked up at the clock.
Aunt Brown-paws was so pleased to see
Willie Wren pop out that she didn't
notice that the hands were
pointing to ten minutes before
four o'clock.

"Four o'clock!" she cried.
"I must catch the bus.
Goodbye, my dears, and thank-you,
Bertha, for such a lovely tea."

"I'm glad the
clock is in such
good order, Barnaby,"
she called out. "The note
of the cuckoo is very strong
and clear."
   Aunt Brown-paws was away
to catch the bus.

Out came Willie from inside the clock
and down flew Charley Cuckoo.
   "Why did you 'cuckoo!' so early?"
asked Barnaby. "It was only ten-to-four.
You could have spoiled everything for us."
   "Your aunt was just going to take
another jam tart," said Charley
in a cross voice, "and the
two that are left are for us!"

Rusty's House

Rusty was a little rabbit and, although he lived in a cosy burrow with his brother and sisters, he wanted some adventures.

"I'm tired of this burrow," he told the other little rabbits,
"I shall go and look for a house of my own."
Flop-ears looked at him with admiring eyes but Brownie said,
"Mummy won't let you."
"I shan't tell her," said Rusty,
"I shall just go."

He waited until the other rabbits were playing
in the warren, then he put on his coat
and quietly tip-toed from the burrow
onto the road.

The sun was shining, the birds were singing and the butterflies were fluttering from flower to flower as the little rabbit wandered along among the trees.

"How beautiful the world is!" said Rusty. "I'm glad I decided to leave the burrow."

And then a little figure with a long tail
ran across the path; she wore a
jacket and skirt and a large bonnet.
    "Hello, Mandy Mouse!" cried Rusty.
"I'm looking for a house of my own;
I've left home and I'm going to live
by myself."

Mandy Mouse looked surprised.
"I thought all little rabbits lived in a burrow,"
she said, "and yours is such a cosy one."
"I'm tired of it," Rusty said, "it's too crowded;
it will be much nicer to have a house of my own."

"Come with me," said Mandy, "there is a fine house for sale in the old oak tree – perhaps you would like to live there."

So off they went through the woods.

There was a FOR SALE sign
over one of the oak tree houses;
these looked very pretty and were close to
the woodland shop.

"Very handy," Mandy pointed out, "they sell
almost everything."

"It looks nice," agreed Rusty, "I'll go inside and look around."

It was a rather tight squeeze but at last he got through the doorway.

There was a long dark passage inside that Rusty
didn't like very much and the rooms were so tiny
that he could hardly turn round.

"It's very small; I don't think I would
like to live here," he said.

He thanked Mandy and told her that, since he would probably grow into a much fatter rabbit than he was already, he must look for a bigger house.

So Mandy went off to do her shopping and Rusty wandered away through the woods.

The next person he met was Filbert, the squirrel,
and they walked along together.
"The trees are the best places to live in," said Filbert,
"why don't you build yourself a big comfortable nest
or choose a hole in a tree and make a house
there?"
"That's a good idea," agreed Rusty, "but I'm not sure
if I could build a nest or climb a tree."

"Try this one," suggested Filbert, "there's a nice, big hole up there." Rusty's feet were not made for climbing but, with Filbert's help, he managed to reach the hole.

"Tu-whit-tu-who's this?"
hooted an angry voice.
Out of the hole popped
Oscar Owl.
    Rusty was so scared
that he let go of the branch
he was holding
and came tumbling down
on top of Filbert.

"I hope I didn't hurt you," said the rabbit
when they had picked themselves up,
"are you all right?"

"Just a little stunned," gasped Filbert,
"I think you'd better find a house closer to the ground;
you are a bit too heavy for tree climbing."

Rusty thanked him and gave him a toffee
that he found in his coat pocket.

He trotted on down the river bank.
There he met Flippy Frog.

"Can you help me?" asked Rusty. "I'm
looking for a house."
"Of course I can," said Flippy,
"I know all the best houses on the river bank.
Quite a number of them are empty at present."

He showed the rabbit some riverside houses
but they were not the type Rusty wanted.
They were very, very damp; in fact,
most of them had deep pools of water
on the floor.

"So refreshing in the hot weather,"
explained Flippy.

Rusty walked along the river bank.
It was very beautiful there; the golden kingcups
were growing in the water and the dragonflies
darted to and fro.

But, although the rushes made a soft swish-swish sound
like music, Rusty was not feeling very happy.

It seemed a long time since he had left home
and his merry little brother and sisters.
He began to feel lonely and the tears
in his eyes made it difficult to see
where he was going.

Suddenly he tripped over a stone, lost his balance and fell – plop – into the river!

Oh, how cold it was! How rough it was!

The water rushed along, past big boulders, carrying the little rabbit with it.

He tried to struggle to the bank
but the river swept him
under a bridge and past a
water-wheel on and on.

"I can't swim!" cried Rusty.
"Oh, what shall I do!"

Some little fish popped out of
the water as he floated by,
but they were much too small
to help him.

And then he heard a friendly "Moo!" and there
on the bank stood a big brown and white cow.
    She put her feet into the water and gently
grabbed the bunny with her mouth.
Rusty was lifted out of the river and
tossed on to the grass.
    "I've seen some funny things
floating down the river," declared the cow,
"but you're the funniest. Did you fall in
or were you just enjoying a swim?"

Rusty told his adventures and the cow nodded her head wisely.

"Cheer up!" she mooed. "I know of a house that will suit you exactly."

Rusty walked by her side, his wet clothes leaving a trail behind him.

It was getting late and he was cold and hungry; he did hope he would find a house before dark.

"Run through the trees," said the cow, "turn to the right and you'll see a lovely little house. You can't miss it."